CUB

CUB

Paul Coccia

orca soundings

ORCA BOOK PUBLISHERS

Library and Archives Canada Cataloguing in Publication

Coccia, Paul, 1982–, author
Cub / Paul Coccia.
(Orca soundings)

Issued in print and electronic formats.
ISBN 978-1-4598-2082-1 (softcover).—ISBN 978-1-4598-2083-8 (PDF).—
ISBN 978-1-4598-2084-5 (EPUB)

I. Title. II. Series: Orca soundings
PS8605.O243C83 2019   jc813'.6   C2018-904691-0
C2018-904692-9

First published in the United States, 2019
Library of Congress Control Number: 2018954081

Summary: In this high-interest novel for teen readers, Theo enters a
cooking contest and catches the eye of a celebrity restaurant owner.

*Orca Book Publishers is dedicated to preserving the environment and
has printed this book on Forest Stewardship Council® certified paper.*

Orca Book Publishers gratefully acknowledges the support for its
publishing programs provided by the following agencies: the Government of
Canada, the Canada Council for the Arts and the Province of British Columbia
through the BC Arts Council and the Book Publishing Tax Credit.

Edited by Tanya Trafford
Cover images by iStock.com/ParkerDeen (front) and
Shutterstock.com/Krasovski Dmitri (back)

ORCA BOOK PUBLISHERS
orcabook.com

Printed and bound in Canada.

22 21 20 19 • 4 3 2 1

To Mom and Xavier,
my companions in the kitchen.

Chapter One

"I'm just not going to apply," I tell Di as I punch down my bread dough. It needs a second rise. With a few hits, it deflates. I look at my belly and wish I could do the same. Make it go from soft and squishy to washboard abs that would make other guys take notice. And maybe ask me out. I should probably do some sit-ups or crunches, whatever

1

those are, to make that a reality. I'm not really big into sports or fitness.

Di waves her arms in the air. She looks like a crow flapping. Her latest outfit has a lot of flowing, black material. The micro braids pinned on top of her head like a giant nest only add to the image. Plus Di is tall, taller than most of our teachers, so the nest looks like it's way up in a tree.

I'm tall too. It's how we first saw each other the first day of high school, literally over the heads of the entire class. Di says it was a sign. I said it was genetics. Plus all the growth hormones in dairy products. She said we were friends. And we are.

"Theo, you have to," she says. "It's an amazing opportunity. And as your hag—"

"You're not my hag," I interrupt. "I hate when you call yourself that.

We don't have to be clichés. We can be best friends and that's it."

Di rolls her eyes. "Same thing. As I was saying, you know I'm always right. I said you should try to get into the school's baking program. Now you're the star of it."

"I don't know about star," I say. She's right though. She insisted I apply to this program. It's very selective and elite. But I got in. Di knows I love being in the kitchen, the feel of dough under my hands, the smells, the decorating, the tastes, the goodies at the end of it all. The problem is, I can't help eating the delicious results. I'm sure when guys look at me they see a huge giant. A big, fat gay guy who bakes. It's the recipe for a joke. And I'm the punch line.

"You don't have any confidence. That's your only problem," says Di.

Di is the opposite. She drips confidence. She is a plus-size diva, proud of her curves and stature. When she couldn't find the kind of clothing she wanted to wear, she started sewing. That landed her a spot in our school's fashion program. She has even sold some of her designs and runs a small online business.

"At least look at the application," Di says pushing the printout at me. "It's at HEAT, the hottest restaurant in town. And you could win a ton of cooking equipment and a whack of cash. Which you will totally need when you get into culinary school."

"If I get in."

"*When*. And you actually know how to use the equipment! How cool would it be to cook in a real restaurant?"

"If I get in," I repeat.

"When," Di repeats. "And are you forgetting who owns HEAT?"

Kyle Carl Clark, or KCC, as he's called, just happens to be my favorite Toronto chef. I see him all the time doing interviews and cooking segments on TV and in magazines. He opens one trendy restaurant after another, each one a success. It doesn't hurt that he looks like a model with his broad chest, muscled arms and scruffy, salt-and-pepper facial hair. His restaurants are hot. So is he.

It's annoying how often Di is right. I would be an idiot not to take advantage of this opportunity.

"And it's down on Church Street, right in the middle of the Village," Di continues. "The *Gay* Village. Your people! This cooking competition has your name written all over it. You need to apply."

I take the paper and sigh. I've seen it already. It popped up on my phone's feed last night. I actually considered entering.

Everything about the competition is tempting. But I decided that I can't do it.

"I can't," I say, trying to hand the paper back to her.

"Can't or won't? Give me a reason. A good one."

"It's a cooking competition. I'm a baker."

"You cook all the time," Di says, waving my excuse away with her hand. "Your food is great. Next?"

"I'm too young."

"There wasn't any mention of age restrictions. And seventeen is hardly too young. Try again."

"My mom won't like the idea."

"I already texted her, and she's cool. I told her it wouldn't get in the way of classes."

I hate that Di is friends with my mom. They shouldn't even have each other's numbers.

I dust flour off my apron. "Look at me," I say. Di rolls her eyes again. I keep talking. "I'm chunky. You know how judgy gay guys can be." Someone at school actually told me I should think about getting an eating disorder if I want to get laid. I pretended I didn't hear. Yeah, people can be jerks, but I can't deny I should probably lose some weight. I just need to look at myself or grab a handful of my flab to know it's true. "I don't want everyone looking at me."

Di looks me up and down. "The problems with your body are in your head. You're cuddly, like a teddy bear. With a lot of muscle from all the kneading and lifting you do in here. If I was a guy, I'd be all over you."

She sees teddy bear. I see whale. Anyway, it doesn't matter if Di says she'd date me. She's not a guy. She doesn't understand gay-guy weight standards at all.

Di hasn't finished. "I'm fatter than you, and I'm in fashion. Yes, the industry is built on appearance. But I'm not going to let a bunch of judgy bitches hold me back. You can't either. Especially if you're planning to open up bakeries across the city. Soon everyone will know your face and your baking."

I cover my dough with plastic wrap. I do want to open a bakery. Then, all going well, maybe a chain of them. One day I'll have the perfect business, the perfect body (slim and toned, with no flab) and the perfect guy who is crazy about me. Everything will fall into place.

"Right now I'm the Pillsbury Dough Boy. You're different than me, Di. You're not afraid to take crazy chances," I say. Her outfits alone make that clear.

"But you try new things all the time when you bake," Di persists.

"That's not the same. You can eat your mistakes, and then they're gone. Baking is the one thing I feel good about. I don't want to get rejected and end up feeling bad about myself or worse about my looks. And I definitely don't want to start feeling bad about my baking. I know I should be cooler about everything, but I'm not there yet. I've decided."

Di gives me a huge grin, "I knew you'd be like this."

"I'm not like anything."

Di keeps grinning. "You are. You don't believe in yourself. But I believe in you. That's why I already sent in your application." She waits for me to close my mouth before she says, "You can thank me with brownies."

I pull the tea towel free from my apron and tug it between both hands. "You did what?" I chase Di around the counter. "I'm not making you brownies. I'm making you a noose!" For a bigger girl, she can move fast.

She laughs as she darts out the door. "The soy-caramel brownies," she calls over her shoulder. "I love those."

Chapter Two

I do end up making some brownies.
My regular gooey fudgy ones. And
I make sure the other students in the
baking program eat most of them. I save
Di only the tiniest dried-out piece from
the corner of the pan. I don't want her
thinking she did something good by
entering me in the contest, even if she

means well. Anyway, the odds are good I won't make it in.

A week goes by. I bake Di an entire pan of soy-caramel brownies. She and I eat them together, because while I didn't think I'd make it into the contest, I did kind of hope I might.

"It's too soon to hear," Di says. "These brownies are amazing. Soy instead of salt. Brilliant." She licks the caramel off her fingers. "Don't give up yet."

Another week goes by. I still don't hear anything.

"They could still call. The competition starts next month," Di says.

"That's only two weeks away," I point out. "They probably have everyone they need by now." I'm playing it cool, but now I realize I'm really hoping to be chosen.

Over the weekend I search online for news on the contest. There's none.

By Monday I've given up all hope. By Tuesday I'm disappointed but all right. By Wednesday life is back to normal. I'm going to classes, doing my homework, baking.

After class my phone rings. It's a blocked number, so I don't answer. My hands are covered with melted chocolate anyway.

Whoever calls doesn't leave a message. Then my phone rings again. And again. By the fifth call I'm kind of annoyed but also worried there's an emergency or something. I rinse off my hands and answer. "Hello?"

"Is this Theo Childs?" The voice is high-pitched.

"Who's asking?"

"Theo who applied for HEAT's cooking contest?"

My heart starts pounding. "Yes. This is Theo."

"Great. I'm calling about HEAT's contest. Duh! Right?"

I laugh a little, not sure how to respond.

"So they liked your application, and I'm calling to ask you to come in for an interview. You'll need to bring something for us to taste. Does this Friday afternoon work? I know it's short notice, but the competition starts soon. Between three and four? Come to the restaurant. Cool?"

"I'll be there."

"Sweet. I'll send an email with more info. Bye now!" *Click.*

I text Di to meet me in the cooking lab. She gets there as I finish dipping the truffles into the chocolate.

"I told you," Di says when I tell her about the interview. "I told you! What are you going to make? One of your awesome cakes?"

I shake my head. My cakes are impressive, but they're not right for this. "It's a *cooking* contest. I can't bake my way in."

"But you bake the best stuff," Di says.

"But real chefs cook. Pastry chefs bake. I need to come up with something amazing to cook. I need to brainstorm."

Di claps. Her arms are loaded almost to her elbows with thin bangles that tinkle. "So start thinking! What do you like to cook?"

"I don't know," I say. "I mean, I cook dinner and stuff, but I don't know what's going to wow the interviewers. I need to show skill and creativity, and it needs to taste great."

"How about pasta?"

"Anyone can do pasta. I need more."

"You're great on the grill."

I shake my head. "Grilled food won't travel or reheat well."

But this is helping me narrow it down. I make a list of all the dishes I cook at home.

Di grabs the list and crosses off a bunch of items. I grab it back and cross off more.

We look at what's left.

"What if you took this and combined it with this," Di says, pointing to two different items.

"And added the sauce from here," I say, thinking aloud.

"And get into the competition," Di says. "And win."

Chapter Three

I walk past HEAT again. This makes thirteen times. A baker's dozen. My heart is racing, and I'm sweating. My stomach feels like someone reached in and is squeezing. It grinds against itself in a weird, uncomfortable way, like my guts are trying to tie knots in themselves. I've never had a panic attack. I wonder if this is what one feels like. Ironically, the thought calms me a little.

I'm carrying my interview dish. I'm pretty happy with how it turned out. If nothing else, it smells great. I made sure it reheats well too.

I'm not as worried about my food as I am about the interview. What if they don't like me or I say something stupid? This is an actual restaurant with an actual celebrity chef. Who I might actually meet and who might actually eat my food. There's more to this than cash or prizes. This isn't a classroom or a practice run. This is real life. I have a shot at something real.

I swallow. My stomach gurgles and grinds again. I reach for the door handle of the restaurant and pull it open. If I want a real shot, I have to go for it. But first I have to get inside.

The waitstaff, dressed in black, are wiping down and setting up tables for the dinner rush. The floors, tables and walls are all made of dark wood. Except for the wall behind the bar. It's made of exposed brick with layers of different-colored paint that have been artfully removed. The bar is brushed stainless steel, as are all the chairs. Oversized lightbulbs suspended by thin wires hang over tables. The place looks dark, industrial, modern, urban, fashionable. It looks masculine, intimidating. The whole place reminds me of KCC.

In the back corner is a long table that would seat at least a dozen people. A man and a woman are seated behind it, both in black. Several people are talking to them and handing them plastic containers and pans. Suddenly I find myself looking into the eyes of a bearded man with a full face of glitter makeup. Where did he come from? He is wearing a large wig and beaded dress, complete with chest hair sticking out.

His legs are hairy too, and he has a bit of a beer belly.

"Theo?" he asks. "Theo Childs? You're the last to arrive. I was wondering if that was you pacing out front. I'm Mama Bear, resident drag queen and hostess. Come on in. What did you bring? It smells so good."

Before I can answer, Mama Bear has taken the tinfoil off my dish and dug in. I hadn't noticed he was carrying a fork. Or maybe he'd hid it under his wig.

"That's *amazing*! Wow. The best thing I've eaten all day. But what is it?" he asks.

"Crepe enchiladas with a pesto–green-chili sauce. It's French-Latin fusion," I say as Mama Bear takes another bite.

"A little spicy, a little creamy, a *lot* good. Just right!" Mama Bear declares.

"Thanks." I blush a little. I'm not sure what to think of Mama Bear.

He's not like any drag queen I've seen before. He doesn't look feminine. There's no doubt he's a man, even if his eyelids are covered in glitter. Not to mention the lipstick and heels. I decide he's a fusion too. I like that.

"Blake, Beth, you've got to try this," Mama Bear says as he leads me to the long table.

"Who is this?" Blake says. He lowers his glasses and looks over the rims at me as he waves me toward him.

"It must be Theo Childs," Beth says, looking at a list. She has a very cool haircut, one side long and the other side shaved into a fadeaway. It's edgy and daring. Di would love it.

Blake and Beth look at my application, heads together, then look at me.

"I don't know," Beth says, as if she is answering a question Blake asked but not out loud. "I'm not sure he's what we're going for."

"We're not going for good cooks?" Mama Bear asks.

Blake sighs and speaks as if he's explaining something to a child for the millionth time. "We're creating an image here. A look. We need contestants who fit that. Branding is so important now. He's going to represent us. How he looks says something about who we are. I see a pudgy kid in sneakers and jeans. What's HEAT about you?" he asks, finally looking back at me.

Before I can answer, Mama Bear says, "That's garbage. He'll draw in a younger crowd. He's a big cutie, all tall and cuddly. He will appeal to groups you're not even thinking about. More important, his food is great. He's just right for this contest."

As Mama Bear and the other interviewers argue, I grab plates and forks off a nearby table. I load generous portions onto three plates. As far as looks and image go, I may not be what they're after. But I know if they try my food, I still have a chance.

I put the still-warm food down in front of them. I watch Blake's and Beth's faces change as the aroma of my food reaches them.

Beth almost shyly takes a bite. "Mmm," she says with a sigh.

Blake takes the tiniest bite. His eyes get wide. He takes a bigger bite.

"I told you," Mama Bear says. "Just. Right."

Reaching for another forkful, Blake says, "Mama Bear, food is one thing. But we really do need to consider our contestants as a whole in terms of image and representation. Who we are, who our clients are. Is this kid HEAT?"

"Absolutely. And I'm not going to stop harassing you until you let him into the competition," Mama Bear says, snatching up the third plate. "So what if he's a cub? He's also the best cook we've had today."

When Mama Bear matter-of-factly calls me a cub, I don't mind. I probably would have if Blake or a gay guy from my high school had said it. But I *am* gay, young, husky and a bit furry. I'm not a monster or a giant blob. I'm a cub. It fits.

Blake looks at me and purses his lips. "Fine. I will think about it. Mr. Childs, please fill out this form. We need to know more about you. We'll be in touch."

I reach for the form. All the plates are empty.

Chapter Four

"Hi. This message is for Theo. I think I called you before. Anyway, I'm phoning to let you know that you have been accepted as one of HEAT's competitors. Congratulations! There will be four rounds over the next four Saturdays. Someone will get eliminated each week. Look for an email with more instructions. Oh, one last thing. As well as the cash and prizes, KCC may offer the winner a job at one of his restaurants. Good luck! Bye now."

I find Di working in one of the sewing labs. She's zipping yards of red fabric through the machine, her bare foot working the pedal. She's wearing her canary-yellow catsuit and has kicked off the matching platform shoes.

I tell her about the voice mail.

"This is crazy," I say. "I could end up with a job. With KCC. At one of the best restaurants in the city. This could start my career."

"And who do you have to thank?" Di asks, blinking her lashes at me.

I sigh. "More brownies?"

"We're beyond brownies. Grab that white fabric and put it on the cutting table, will you?"

I grab the bolt. It's a little heavy. I hoist it onto the table.

"We should celebrate," Di says.

"Burgers?" I ask.

"And milkshakes," Di adds.

"And poutine." I probably shouldn't be eating all those carbs. Soon I'm going to be in front of a crowd of people. Blake and Beth already think my looks don't fit HEAT's image.

"*Always* poutine," Di says, laughing. "Without it, how can it be a celebration? I need to finish up something, and then I'm good to go. Give me an hour?"

Di's response makes me feel better instantly. We're going out to celebrate. I don't need to worry about a calorie count for this one meal.

When I go back to get Di, she's hunched over the table. Her mouth is full of pins that she plucks out and jabs into whatever it is she's working on. Her hands smooth out the material in between.

"What's going on?" I ask. I've seen her like this before. When Di is creating, she can be intense.

"Come here," Di mumbles around the pins.

When I'm close, she grabs me and nudges me. "Stand straight," she says, spitting the pins out and dropping them in a clear plastic box. She grabs what she was working on and holds it up against me. "I think it will fit," she says. "But you'd better try it on."

"What is it?" I ask, looking down.

"Your chef whites. You need the white coat. I made you an apron too. You need to look like the real thing."

I try to give her a big hug. Too late, we both remember the pins in the fabric.

We jump apart. I put the coat down onto the table.

"I want you to put that on," Di says.

I grab Di and hug her properly. We're a good size for one another. I'm a bit taller and wider, so she fits snugly against my chest.

"Thanks," I whisper.

Di slides her arms around me. She squeezes back. "One of your bear hugs is a way better thanks than your brownies any day."

Chapter Five

Four stainless-steel cook stations are arranged on a small platform stage. The long table now faces the stations.

Mama Bear, in a silk robe, hurries over to me. He's got streaks of different-colored sparkles through his beard and in his chest hair.

"Hey, I was wondering when the cooking cub would show. We need you backstage." Mama Bear leads me to a curtained-off area near the entrance to the kitchen. When I see the other competitors, I can see exactly why the judges were concerned about my image.

The first contestant is busy on his phone, thumbs flying. He glances up briefly as Mama Bear introduces him: Zack. He's blond and looks like he barely eats, all sinew and bones.

"I'm doing a live feed," Zack says without looking up.

The next contestant, Jeff, works as a personal chef. I'd put him in his thirties. He looks fit under his printed button-down. He shakes my hand before turning away.

Dixon, number three, has muscles on top of muscles. We shake hands. His grip is firm. His forearms bulge with veins.

I must be staring at his arms because Dixon lets go of my hand, then pats my belly. "I'm a personal trainer. If you ever get tired of your muffin top, call me." He holds out his business card.

"Thanks." I shove the card in my pocket quickly. My face burns to the tips of my ears.

"Ignore him. He's a gym bunny," the last contestant says. He has a full head of hair with silver strands running through it. "I'm Dennis. Nice to meet you, Theo." He tells me he's just a home cook.

Blake and Beth enter the curtained-off area.

"Welcome, everybody," says Blake. "So. Each round is going to have a different theme. We'll line you up, Mama Bear will do his hosting thing, and then he'll announce this week's challenge. Then you do your thing. After the judges do their tasting, one of you will be eliminated. Cool?" he asks. He doesn't wait for a reply. "Good luck. We're starting in a few."

I pull my chef's jacket and apron out of my backpack and put them on.

I hear a snicker and look over to catch Jeff and Dixon watching me and talking in low voices.

"Don't pay them any attention. Just do your thing," Dennis says. "Your coat fits you perfectly." He fixes my collar as we line up.

Blake and Beth return as Mama Bear leaves. I hear Beth introducing the competition over the speakers. We are told to walk single file to our stations and not stop to look around or wave.

The last instructions weren't needed. As I walk out, the stage lights make it hard to see anything past the cooking area. As my eyes adjust, I start to make out shapes. Slowly those shapes turn into people.

I hear someone whistle and see fabric swishing like banners. Di is in the front row.

"Welcome, everyone," says Mama Bear. "Before you get started, I want to introduce you to today's judges. They know what it means to be in the line of fire." As Mama Bear tells us their names, I realize I have seen them before. They are servers from HEAT, two girls and a guy.

Introductions done, Mama Bear continues. "Down in the Village, nothing says Sunday like brunch. Chefs, your task today is to update a brunch classic. It should be able to stand up to Saturday night's drinking and be tasty enough that we forget our figures." Mama Bear pushes out his belly and rubs it. "You have one hour. Ready, set, HEAT!"

I take stock of my station as I think about what I like for brunch. My favorite is eggs benedict. I think its various components will show enough skill to get me through to the next round. I make a mean hollandaise sauce and know how to poach an egg perfectly, so it has that sunny, runny yolk. I get my pots going, English muffins split and eggs cracked.

Feeling confident, I think about what to serve on the side. As I wait for my water to come to a simmer, I peek around. Dixon and Jeff both have eggs and English muffins at their stations. They're probably doing eggs benedict too. Damn. Well, it's an obvious choice for brunch.

"A second eggs benedict," Mama Bear confirms as she reaches Dixon's station.

Dixon grins. "Well, mine is going to be healthier than Jeff's. You won't have to pay the price on Monday for Sunday's brunch."

With only five contestants, I can't be the third making the same thing. I look around my station again. I see some cinnamon rolls and a jar of pickles.

With the ham I was going to use with my eggs benny, I can change direction. I'll do a take on a Monte Cristo. The cinnamon rolls look dry enough to really soak up the eggs I have already cracked. And Cuban sandwiches have ham and pickles with a mustard spread. But will these ingredients work together? It's a risk. Combining the sweet cinnamon bread and the spicy mustard with the salty ham and briny pickles could be a genius move. Or a total disaster. I grab a fork and whisk my eggs, then slice the rolls to get them in. I'll deep-fry the buns to give them a crunchy outside and creamy inside.

Mama Bear arrives at my station and asks me a couple of questions. I barely have time to answer him. I'm too busy slicing the ham and pickles and preparing the dipping sauces.

As I finish plating, Mama Bear gives the warning—one minute left. I grab an apple and a pear. I manage to fan the last of the slices onto the plates as the ten-second countdown ends.

I don't know how my sandwich is going to taste, but it sure looks good.

We line up in front of the long table as the judges begin to taste our dishes.

Zack made apple-pie pancakes. The judges say they're a bit sweet but yummy.

Jeff's traditional eggs benedict have some issues. The hollandaise separated, and the eggs are overdone.

Dennis presents mini omelets stuffed with different fillings. They seem to go over well. The judges are impressed with the ambition of one item served three ways.

Dixon made egg-white benedicts with avocado sauce and smoked salmon. They look great, but the judges aren't blown away by the flavor profile. It's lacking something to tie it all together.

The judges get to my sandwich last.

"What is this?" one of them asks. "We thought you were doing an eggs benedict too."

"I was," I admit as another judge looks at my sandwich, lifts the top and wrinkles her nose when she sees the pickles and mustard. "Then I realized you were already going to eat that. Twice. I decided I'd better make something different. It's a Monte Cristo Cuban sandwich made with cinnamon rolls. There's warm maple syrup with butter and strawberry jam jazzed up with some grapefruit juice for dipping."

The judge who opened the sandwich asks, "I admire your ability to think on your feet. But is this something *you* would eat?"

"I like Monte Cristo and Cuban sandwiches," I say nervously. "So, yeah, I think I'd eat it."

Jeff and Dixon laugh from their spots.

Mama Bear gives them a look. He picks up half of the sandwich from the extra plate, the one we were told was for display only, and takes a big bite. "You *think* you'd eat it? You mean you didn't try it?" he asks.

I shake my head. *Uh-oh*.

Mama Bear pushes the other half of the sandwich at me. "Take a bite."

I take a small bite, everyone watching. I take a second, bigger bite. The flavors totally work and complement each other. It's delicious. Mama Bear takes another bite of his half.

The judges finally dig in.

"I have to stop eating so we can judge," says the one who didn't believe I would eat it myself. "If I'm honest, this seemed like the grossest combination of things. Just the idea of it was disgusting. The problem is, it's disgustingly good."

"I think we have a dark horse," the last judge says.

"It's the type of thing I'd work out all week to eat," the first judge says between bites. "I know we need to make a decision about who is going home today, but all I want to do is finish this sandwich."

After the judges talk among themselves for a few moments, the first judge addresses the five of us.

"With this dish, there were some technical missteps and a lack of creativity. We asked for an update, and we got a flawed classic. Unfortunately, that's not acceptable in this competition. You have to nail every element." She pauses for a moment. "Jeff, I'm afraid you have been eliminated."

I take a deep breath. Changing directions, taking a risk, paid off. I'm still in the game.

"We look forward to seeing the rest of you next week."

Chapter Six

Round two. Even though it's mid-afternoon and there is no food service, the restaurant is packed. Every table is full. People are standing in any empty space available and crowding the bar to buy drinks. Zack told me backstage that his posting about last week's results went viral. There are even reporters in the audience.

Di is sitting with a bunch of people I don't know. I don't think she knows them either. She's wearing a neon tracksuit with huge, fuzzy leg warmers. Her hair is in a high ponytail.

Today there are only two judges seated at the long table, both cooks from HEAT.

With his usual flair Mama Bear announces the theme. "The challenge is date night. Ready, set, HEAT!"

In front of me is a table of cute guys about my age. They all look pretty similar—shorter than me, skinny jeans and tight tees showing off their lean bodies. Awesome high-tops and cool haircuts. One of them smiles at me. I smile back. He winks, then turns to talk to one of his friends.

I'm wasting time. I need to figure out what to make. But there's a big problem. I've never actually been on a date. I wouldn't even know how to ask a guy out. Without any dating experience, I don't know where to even begin. I'm drawing a blank.

If I had someone coming over for dinner, what would I make? Steak and potatoes seems like it would satisfy most guys. It's safe, but it may also get me through to the next round. I grab a bunch of spices and decide to do a rub. I add a bit of coffee to make it more interesting. I throw some baking potatoes in the microwave to give them a head start. I will double-stuff them with some cheese, bacon and more spices. I get some peas and carrots roasting. The last thing I do before I focus on cooking my steak perfectly is mix up a quick Irish soda bread and pop it in the oven. Homemade bread should impress a date and the judges too.

The only sounds are the audience chatting and Mama Bear on the speaker, providing a play-by-play. The other contestants are quiet.

I glance up to see Di and the guy who winked watching me.

I pull my steaks from the grill. They have the marks I want and need to rest so the insides are nice and juicy. The potatoes have crisp tops, and the vegetables glisten.

My plates look like they came from a high-end steakhouse when I send them off. While I have no experience dating, I am hoping this meal would land me a second date and will get me another week in the competition.

"Before the judging starts," Mama Bear says, "you may have noticed there's an empty seat at the judges' table. Well, you all know our next judge. And he will be a permanent fixture in the competition going forward. Please welcome the chef himself, Kyle Carl Clark, owner of HEAT."

The crowd claps enthusiastically as a spotlight clicks on. KCC strides into it. He looks even better in person. He's sporting a leather motorcycle jacket and white T-shirt. His square jaw has a little scruff and his hair has a touch of gray. His smile gleams. He gives a wave as he struts to the table.

"I've heard good things about you guys," KCC says as he takes his spot. "Let's see which one of you men would cook your way into my heart." He winks. "Or my bedroom."

The audience giggles. I do too, even though I am thinking of all the great bakers in my class and all the famous chefs who are women. I wonder if women didn't apply to the contest or if they weren't chosen because they didn't fit with HEAT's "image."

Zack is first up.

"Is this what you'd make for me on a date?" KCC asks him.

Zack, phone in hand, shrugs. "I'm not sure I'd be inviting anyone to my house on a first date. It's not the best choice for personal safety. Cold cases are so not hot."

Everyone is silent. Then KCC laughs. And then everyone joins in, myself included.

I'm up next. I don't even register what the judges say to Zack. I'm hoping KCC gets the best plate out of the four. I'm too busy obsessing to listen.

"I've been hearing lots about you, Theo," KCC says as my steak is placed in front of him. "The way to a man's heart is supposed to be through the stomach. From what I've heard, you should be able to cook me right out of my pants."

"Yes, sir," I respond. My mouth drops open. I can't believe I just said that. The audience laughs hard. I open my mouth several more times, trying to think of something to correct what I said.

"Sir, eh? That might help with my pants." KCC smiles. The audience laughs again.

As they finish tasting, the first cook says, "It's good but not really original."

The second cook nods. "I agree. Steak and potatoes. It's standard, although you did dress it up nicely. I'm more impressed by the bread, considering the time limit. But I'm not sure I'd want this heavy a meal on a date."

"Me either," the first cook agrees.

"Well," KCC says, "it may not be original, but I think most guys would be quite impressed if you made this for them on a first date and made it this well."

"It's safe. Safe was cut last week. The contestants need to think outside the box. Where's the creativity?" the first cook asks.

KCC takes another bite of my steak. "It is a bit expected, even the coffee-spice rub. But it tastes great. The meat is cooked right. The potato is tasty. The bread is awesome. This kid has skills some chefs twice his age don't. We should factor that in."

"But would it get your pants off?" the first cook asks.

KCC grins. "Naughty, naughty. I'll be in trouble if I answer that. All I'll say is, I would definitely stay for dessert."

My stomach feels like it has tied itself into the grinding knots again. My food was unoriginal. KCC was nice about it, but he called my dish *expected*. I might be out, and if I am, I don't have a shot at a job. Worse, KCC, the chef I'm crazy about, doesn't think I'm creative. Whatever small reputation I have gained, I've messed up. I'll end up a line cook or frosting cakes at the back of some no-name bakery.

I'm so focused on my inner critic that I only tune in when I realize Dixon is arguing with the judges. "It's meant to be good for you. All the antioxidants will get your blood pumping. You'll be energized and have stamina. That's what you want on a good date."

KCC looks at Dixon hard. "I'll ask you the question again. Is this a sexy plate of food?"

Dixon huffs. "Looking good and feeling good *is* sexy."

The judges talk to one another and keep motioning between my plate and Dixon's.

KCC clears his throat. "So we've had some disagreement. Theo, after last week we expected more from you. Your plate was cooked to perfection but lacked inspiration. Dixon, your creativity was impressive, but a healthy meal isn't really first-date material. So our decision came down to which plate we'd finish eating. On that we agreed. Theo..."

I gulp and clasp my hands together as I stare directly into KCC's eyes.

"...we will see you next week."

My stomach gives a final grind before it releases. I close my eyes and take a deep breath. KCC would finish eating my dinner. I have another chance.

"Total garbage," Dixon mumbles beside me.

I check my phone. Di has been blowing it up with texts. I text her.

I'm ok, talk later, gonna pack up.

I grab my pack from backstage. As I'm about to leave, I hear my name.

"Theo should have gone," Dixon says. "Especially since last week you got kicked out for the same reason. It's stupid. My meal was healthy. That's why I'm out. It wouldn't hurt Theo to eat something healthy."

Jeff and Dixon are by the bar.

"That's so true," Jeff says. "Obviously he knows how to cook. Look at him. He has to be eating something."

"Or everything," Dixon says.

"What's all that crap about trying to give HEAT a certain image? They kicked out the two hottest guys and left the old guy and the fatty."

"Did you see the way Theo was huffing and sweating all over his station?" Dixon says. "It's probably the most exercise he's had in a long time."

"And when he moves around, he probably doesn't know his ass crack and his gut hang out. I'm pretty sure that's a health-code violation. His butt should wear a hairnet."

"He's a little porker," Dixon says with a nod. "Well, not little."

They both laugh.

A lump has lodged in my throat, which has gone dry. I feel tears threatening, not just because of what I overheard, but also because somewhere inside me is a voice saying the same things, telling Jeff and Dixon they're right, telling me no one could ever care for me because I'm fat and ugly. I'm some huge monster as I jiggle around the kitchen, hairy and sweaty. It doesn't matter how well I cook or how hard I compete. I'm just a fat gut and big ass. I rub the back of my hand across my eyes, willing myself not to cry, willing the voice to shut up.

A red light the size of a pin glints in the tears forming at the corners of my eyes. Zack is holding his phone, its red light on. He's been filming everything. He's got me on camera about to cry. He's probably sending it out to his followers, so all the internet can join in and laugh.

I turn and race through the kitchen and out the staff entrance to the back alley behind HEAT. I stop. A motorcycle blocks my way, KCC astride it.

"Sorry," I say as I try to step past. "I didn't know anyone was back here."

KCC grabs my arm. "You look upset. I hope it's not over the stupid contest."

I shake my head.

"What's going on?" KCC asks.

Before I can stop myself, I tell him what I overheard. It all comes spilling out. When I'm done, I feel embarrassed that I unloaded onto KCC of all people. I must seem pathetic.

"I should go," I say. "I almost lost, and now I sound like a loser."

"They're jealous, bitter, bitchy old queens," KCC says without letting go of my arm. "You've got a target on you because you beat them. You have talent. You're going to be successful. You're a threat in this competition, and they're trying to take you down."

"I nearly went down today."

"But you didn't. You'll do better next week. I know you will. And what they said isn't true. You looked good up there. Cute. Sexy, even."

My cheeks are on fire. My ears burn. The hottest of hot chefs, KCC, thinks I'm cute and sexy?

"You were in your element. I wasn't the only one who noticed. Didn't you see your fans?" KCC asks.

If possible, my face gets hotter. "I don't have fans."

"You do. And I'm one." KCC reaches into the side bag and tosses me a helmet. "Get on. I'll give you a ride."

I put on the helmet and get behind KCC. I hug his muscled torso as he drives. My body presses against his. I hold tighter to him on corners. At a stop sign KCC squeezes my knee. I can smell him when we stop—leather and something musky, manly, like the woods. It mixes with the motorcycle exhaust.

I thank him when we get to my place. KCC hugs me. I hold on. I want the moment here with KCC to last a bit longer. KCC doesn't let go, so I keep hugging him. His scent surrounds me. I take a deep breath.

"Feel better?" he whispers in my ear.

I'm suddenly aware of how close he is. "A little, actually. Thanks to you," I whisper back. Dixon and Jeff are far away. Even Zack and his video fade. Right now everything is KCC.

He loosens his hold. I do too. I stare into his eyes. He smiles, then grabs the back of my neck and pulls me in. I don't try to resist. His mouth covers mine. I feel his tongue at my lips and open to let him slide in. My heart is beating in my temples. I'm kissing Chef KCC.

When we break apart, I realize KCC's hand has slid down my back. He's squeezing my butt.

"Don't listen to those guys. They might not appreciate your ass, but if it were on the menu, you'd win without ever turning on the stove."

"It's fat," I say. I bite my bottom lip and look away.

"It's good and fat," KCC says. He gives my ass a slap.

It hurts a little. I like it.

Chapter Seven

On Thursday KCC calls an emergency meeting. I have no idea what this is about. I'm the first one to arrive at HEAT.

Zack comes in next. I don't know how to avoid him. He sees me and heads over. I don't have time to run to the washroom to hide.

"I need to explain," he says as he approaches. "The video is all over."

"What?" I worried about this briefly between thoughts about kissing KCC. People are probably watching the video and laughing at me. Everything Jeff and Dixon said is out there now. And able to be replayed over and over again.

"No, no. It's not like that," Zack says. "Sure, when I heard those guys trashing you, I started filming. But I edited the video and put it online to expose them. What they said wasn't cool. Everyone agrees. Look at the comments. They're all on your side."

Zack hands me his phone. The video has been reposted a lot of times. The only negative comments are about Dixon and Jeff. The rest are supportive of me, saying how they hope I win and show those two what it means to be a winner.

"I wanted to explain, but you ran off. I never meant to make you worry," Zack says as I hand back his phone.

"I was worried," I reply.

"Don't be," he says. "Jeff and Dixon can say whatever they want. They're out. You're not."

Dennis and Mama Bear arrive. We are called into KCC's office. It is a small room with a desk and computer, two chairs and a leather couch. We all sit down.

"So I know you're all wondering why I called you here," says KCC, leaning against the desk, looking as cool as ever. "Thanks largely to Zack's online presence, the competition has blown up. It's bigger than we even hoped, and we've decided to make some changes. I talked it over with staff. We're swamped with reservation requests.

"So the first big change is, we're selling tickets to the competition. Second, we've decided to give it our prime spot on Saturday night. You three will be cooking on our busiest night of

the week instead of between services."
KCC pauses for a moment before
revealing the most surprising part. "As
of right now, we're sold out, no standing
room."

KCC continues to detail the changes.
I stare at his lips and think about how
just a couple of days ago I was kissing
them. The couch smells like him.

KCC ends the meeting. He tells
me to stick around for a few minutes.
I leave with the rest of the contestants
and linger by the office door. Mama
Bear pulls me over to the bar. He looks
completely different out of his dress and
wig.

"Do you know why KCC told you to
stay?" he asks.

"No," I answer, although I have
suspicions and hopes.

Mama Bear frowns. "Just be careful
with him. Okay? Especially when
you're alone."

"Sure," I say as KCC opens his door and calls me. I hurry in, excited to be alone with him.

KCC sits on the couch. He pats the seat beside him. I sit.

"I wanted to make sure you're good after everything," KCC says.

"I'm good," I say with a smile. "I felt much better after our chat."

"Me too," KCC says. "I wanted to talk to you more. You want to be a chef, right?"

"A pastry chef," I say. "I want to open up bakeries."

"I could help with that. You could win this competition. There'd be a job at HEAT for you. You could see how a kitchen runs. I'd like seeing you run around here too. You'd be a great addition to the staff."

"Really?"

"For sure. But it's a lot of hard work. It's not just the food and cooking you need to know. Anyone can learn that. It's the whole thing. The atmosphere. The experience. The nuts and bolts of a business. I can help you learn that too," KCC says. He puts his hand on my thigh and begins rubbing.

I put my hand on top of KCC's. He moves it to his chest. I stroke his chest hair. It is bristly and tickles my palm. He leans in close. I kiss him along his jawline as he explains how much to mark up food and how to calculate overheads.

The door to KCC's office opens. I jump up.

"Brandon, seriously, you don't knock anymore?" KCC says.

Brandon looks professional in dress pants, shiny, pointy-toed black shoes and a crisp, pressed dress shirt.

"It's my office too," Brandon replies. "What were you boys up to in here?"

"Brandon's my partner," KCC says.

"Oh. I'm Theo." I avoid looking directly at Brandon.

"The cub from the contest," KCC adds.

Brandon nods.

"KCC was telling me about costs." It's the only thing I can think of to say.

"Brandon's the numbers guy in our relationship," KCC says. "Maybe he should join us. Sit back down, Theo."

I follow KCC's orders, although I don't really understand. Brandon sits on the arm of the couch, sandwiching me between his knee and KCC.

"It must be cool to work with KCC," I say.

Brandon laughs. "When I don't want to kill him. Don't let him fool you. He's not easy to work with. He's even harder to live with."

I'm confused. "You live together?" I ask. "Like roommates?"

KCC laughs now. "If it were the 1950s. We're partners. Husbands."

I stand up again. "Oh my god. I didn't know. I'm so sorry," I say, looking from Brandon to KCC as realization hits me. "If I had known, I wouldn't have..." I can't believe Brandon's not angry after walking in on me kissing his husband.

Brandon puts his hand on my arm. "Sit down. It's okay. KCC said you'd interest me."

"What?" I ask.

Brandon strokes my arm. KCC reaches out and pats my ass.

I squirm. It's not that I don't like KCC touching me. It just feels weird knowing he's married and his husband is right there.

"Sit down," Brandon repeats. "It's okay. Let's talk numbers. Two plus one."

I don't sit down, not really sure what Brandon and KCC are talking about. "What?" I ask.

Brandon and KCC stand up.

"Maybe this will help explain," Brandon says. He leans in and kisses me.

Before I can respond, KCC turns my head. He kisses me too.

Brandon moves his mouth to my neck.

"Oh. Two plus one. Three," I say into KCC's mouth.

KCC pulls back. Brandon's mouth is on mine again.

"Business is often who you know," KCC says as he kisses me again.

A part of me doesn't believe this is happening. A part of me is cheering me on. I'm kissing not one, but two handsome, successful men. They're even willing to help me and my career. And one of the guys is KCC, a chef and celebrity I've crushed on for ages. This is a fantasy scenario. A part of me really likes kissing them and feeling their lips on my neck, their tongues licking my earlobes, their hands stroking my sides. I kiss them back.

But a part of me wants to leave the office right this second. That part nags at me after the three of us finish making out. It reminds me they're married. It tells me I just met them. It tells me Mama Bear said to be careful, especially alone with KCC.

KCC and Brandon say they'll see more of me again soon.

I give them each a kiss goodbye.

Chapter Eight

"You did *what*?" Di asks. She's wearing a fringed dress made from dollar-store shower curtains. Mama Bear sees her as he walks by, looks her up and down, then gives her a thumbs-up. She returns it.

"Shhh," I tell her. We're in HEAT, and the third round is about to begin. "I don't want everyone to know. Zack could be filming."

Di shakes her head. "As your hag—"

"You're not my hag."

Di continues, "I'm behind you going porn star."

"Seriously, Di!"

"You *should* kiss guys. A lot of them. But you went from never kissing a guy to kissing two older ones. Are you sure you're ready for this?"

"Completely," I say, knowing I'm lying. "They're both hot. They both like me. They offered me help. And it's KCC, *the KCC*."

"They're married. To each other. They don't need a boyfriend."

"It doesn't need to be like that. It's just some kissing. And I liked it. They're good kissers."

"Because you have so much experience there."

"Any louder and we'll need to get you a mic. Thanks for broadcasting my sexual history."

"There's nothing to broadcast. It's not like you're a big stud." She grabs my arm and looks at me. "Theo, are you sure this isn't a big deal? You're not one to take risks. In baking, yes. In life, not really."

"I'm good. They're good guys." My stomach grinds a bit. "It's all going to be fine. Better than fine. It's like a dream. Two super-hot older guys want me."

"Except you've been feeling so shitty about yourself. Suddenly these two guys are hitting on you and being nice and promising to do stuff for you," Di says. "I don't want to ruin anything, but—"

"Then don't," I say. "I'm going to see where it goes. They're cool and attractive and powerful, and yeah, I don't know why, but they're into me."

"Fine," Di says. "But you should be careful."

"Everyone's telling me to be careful. Being careful nearly got me cut from this contest. Taking risks got me noticed. What do you know?"

I can see by Di's face that I shouldn't have said that last part. We stand there not saying anything for a while. It's almost showtime.

"You're on soon. You'd better go get ready," Di says and leaves to take her seat.

The restaurant is full, as many tables as can fit crammed in whether they fit the décor or not. Even the bar is packed. There's no standing room. The servers can barely move among the crowd.

I'm already sweating. My heart is beating fast. This is the most people I have ever been in front of. And I have to perform, to cook, to prove that I deserve a spot in the finals. I barely scraped through last time. This time I need to show KCC I have talent. I need to prove that I deserve his attention, his help, his respect. I need to be creative, risky, unexpected. I want him to see me as a top chef. Even if I'm eliminated today, I want to go out letting him know that I earned my place here and that he didn't make out with some loser. I don't want him thinking he shouldn't have put his faith in me.

Mama Bear calls us out. Zack, Dennis and I wave at the cheering crowd as we take our places.

"HEAT's very own Hungry Games!" Mama Bear declares. "That, by the way, is what I call my pizza order after the show. I'm serious. The staff all wonder who will live to deliver another day. But enough about me. Tonight's theme is… late-night snack plates!"

As soon as I hear the theme, I relax a little. I love whipping up quick and delicious snacks after I've spent the day baking. This is like a jacked-up appetizer round. That satisfying last bite before you fall into bed.

Mama Bear holds his hands in the air, his bushy armpits spilling over the top of his evening gown. "Wait. There's a twist. All these lovely people paid to be here tonight. We want them to get their money's worth. So your task is to present not only the four required plates, but to feed the entire audience. Then they will vote. And those votes will count. But don't worry. We are giving you double your prep time and two assistants. One of your choice and one volunteer."

Di is at my station before I can call her. She pulls off her outfit. Underneath she's in a tank and cutoffs. I open my mouth, ready to apologize.

Di shakes her head. "That's over. Let's do this," she says.

When it's time for an audience member to volunteer, I see arms waving from a table of the same cute guys from last week. The one who winked at me is saying, "Me! Pick me! I volunteer as a tribute! Team Theo!"

He nearly skips up to my station.

"Hi," I say. "Um, thanks for your enthusiasm."

He grabs my hand and shakes it. "I'm Benji. The pleasure is all mine. My friends and I think you're the best."

Mama Bear calls, "Ready, set, HEAT!"

Di, Benji and I huddle.

"We don't have a lot of time," I say, taking the lead. My nerves have calmed. This is my territory. When I'm in the kitchen, I'm in control. "I've done this type of thing before when I've been assigned cafeteria duty. We have a lot of people to feed, so we need to keep things simple but extremely tasty."

"So what are you thinking we could do?" Benji asks.

"Nachos," I answer.

"Is that enough?" Di asks. "Creativity, remember."

I nod and grin. "Slumber-party nachos."

Di smiles too. "Oh. My. God. Yes. You're winning."

Benji looks confused. "What do these nachos do? Watch horror movies and talk about boys until 3 AM? Or is 'sleepover' code for going out clubbing and stumbling home before dawn?" He laughs. It's loud and escapes almost like he's barking. He covers his mouth and looks embarrassed. I think it's sweet.

Di laughs too. "He makes fried won tons stuffed with ground chicken and veggies cooked in a ginger soy sauce. Then he loads them up with nacho stuff like melted cheese and shredded lettuce. Oh! And the hoisin, siracha and lime sauce he drizzles over is insane. They're *so* good." She's almost drooling.

"Perfect for a horror flick then," Benji says.

"Yep," I say before going into command mode. "We'll do this like an assembly line. I'll man the fryer. Di, you get the plates counted. Benji, you'll prep the toppings. After you get plate numbers, Di, preheat the ovens, get the plates warming, and see what cheeses we have. Then you can help Benji. I'll make the sauce and be manning the fryer and the stove. I'll be shouting out orders as we go so keep an ear out. Okay, let's do this!"

Di looks shocked. She only ever sees me in the kitchen working alone, not giving orders.

"Team Theo!" Benji cheers as he grabs an armful of vegetables and heads to the sink to rinse them. Once he starts chopping I notice he's using the wrong knife to hack at a red pepper.

I go over and hand Benji a larger knife. I stand behind him and show him how to hold the knife properly. I put my hand over his and help him cut the pepper into strips. "Easier now, right?"

Benji gulps. "Definitely," he says. I head back to my station.

After that, Benji keeps brushing against me as he preps. He answers everything with "Yes, Chef!" It makes me smile. I wonder momentarily if he's finding excuses to be near me. Nah. I doubt Benji's interested in me. He's so slim and funny, and he's not bad in the kitchen. I don't think I'm his type. I've seen his friends. We're too different. I'm sure it's only the tight space and my size making him brush against me. I'd like to give it more thought, but I need to stay focused. The won tons are easy to burn. That would be a big setback.

Di and Benji ask for more directions when they finish tasks. They handle heating up the broiler and arranging the dishes for plating. Without being asked, they see jobs and do them. We're working together like a well-oiled machine. When we get the five-minute warning, we rotate the dishes among us for plating, broiling and garnish. I taste the sauce and just before adding the siracha I decide to use wasabi instead. I don't want to get called out for not being creative again. I taste the mix and it's good, but not good enough. I add some honey for a touch of sweetness and a bit of cocoa to hint at a Mexican mole. I give it another taste. My usual sauce is good. This sauce is *great*.

Benji takes care of drizzling the sauce and sour cream while and Di tops the plates of cheese-smothered won tons with scallion and shredded lettuce. I do a final check before handing off to the servers.

"Hot stuff over here!" Benji calls as the final seconds count down. Benji and Di join me in pumping out the last plates.

When the last plates leave our station, I throw my arms around Benji and Di. I pull them in for a hug. "We've got this," I say to them. "I just know it. Thank you."

Di releases me first. She collects her outfit, then checks her reflection in the metal countertop. "There's the confidence I've been waiting to see. Maybe going porn star does that for you," she says as she reapplies her lipstick.

"Porn star?" Benji asks, lifting an eyebrow.

"She's joking," I say. "But she's not funny."

"We should do this again," Benji says. "It was fun."

"You two make a good team," Di says.

"We three," I correct.

"I should get back to my friends," Benji says. "We'll be voting for you."

"You're awesome," I tell him as I give him another hug.

Benji leaves but looks back and smiles over his shoulder. Di reaches for the extra nachos. She shoves some into her freshly painted mouth. Then she shoves some into mine.

"This sauce! she says. "OMG!"

"I know," I mumble through my mouthful of nachos.

After what seems like only a few minutes, Mama Bear addresses the crowd. "Attention, everyone. I've just had word from the judges. We have the results already. Unfortunately, Dennis wasn't able to make enough of his appetizers for the whole audience. Without the audience vote, you're done. I'm sorry, Dennis. We really loved having you here."

Mama Bear pauses. The crowd goes silent. "That means our finalists are Zack and Theo. One of these two talented chefs will be our winner. Don't forget to get your tickets for the finale here at HEAT." Lots of cheering and clapping.

Di squeals and squeezes me. When she lets go, I feel someone grab me and turn me around. Benji is bouncing up and down. He wraps his arms around my middle, his face against my chest.

Benji lets go as KCC and Brandon arrive. Brandon hugs me, then KCC. Benji, now behind KCC and Brandon, waits a minute before he steps out of the cooking area. I look over KCC's shoulder at Benji. I smile at him and give a little wave. He gives me a big grin and a bigger wave back.

As he hugs me, KCC whispers in my ear. "Time to celebrate. Get rid of your friend. Meet us in my office. Be discreet."

As KCC lets go and Brandon nods at me, I feel a bit like throwing up. It must be the excitement.

Chapter Nine

I knock on the office door. No one answers. I open it to see KCC sitting at his desk. Brandon stands behind him.

KCC gets up, walks over to me, then pushes the door shut. "Congratulations, cub. You're a finalist. You knew you'd make it. Didn't you?" he says with a big smile.

"I thought I would. I hope you were impressed," I answer.

Brandon says, "Let's celebrate." He pulls a bottle of champagne from behind his back, pops the cork, then fills three glasses lined up on the desk. KCC sits on the couch. He pulls me down beside him. Brandon hands us each a glass.

"To you," KCC says, "and to impressing me."

We clink glasses. I take a sip. It makes my nose itch, so I put it down. KCC throws his head back and drains his. Brandon takes a mouthful as he sits.

"You looked good up there," Brandon says.

"You were in your zone, weren't you?" KCC asks. "Like a younger me. You own the kitchen. You know what's yours, and you're not afraid to take it."

"Yes, Chef," I say. "Sorry. I mean, yes, KCC."

"Don't worry," KCC says. "I like it. It makes me feel like the boss. Are you ready to take orders?" KCC pours himself another glass and drains that one too. He hands me my glass. I take another sip before I put it down again. It tickles less this time.

"What other rooms do you work like that?" Brandon asks. "The bedroom maybe?" He slides his arm over my shoulders and massages them. It feels nice.

I lean against him. "I'm not really experienced there," I admit. I pick up my glass and take another sip. It stills tickles.

KCC slides his hand up to the back of my head. "We can always help with that."

The two men are close. I can smell the champagne on their breath mixing with the leather of the couch and their cologne—Brandon's is more floral than

KCC's musk. I take another sip. I start to feel like I'm getting lost in them, soaked through with them.

I turn my head toward KCC, trying to think of something to say about tonight's competition. I don't get a chance. He kisses me. His hand slides from the back of my head and grips my jaw. When he's done, he turns my face to Brandon. Brandon kisses me too.

"I think you liked that," Brandon says when we break apart and KCC lets go of me.

I lean in instantly and kiss him again. "Yes," I say. I turn to KCC for another kiss. He responds, and when we break apart I can feel where his lips were on mine and where his stubble scratched against me.

Brandon rubs my thigh and KCC strokes my chest as the two men lean across me. They kiss one another, soft and passionate at first, then with an intensity that is almost aggressive. I like watching them as they kiss. I undo two buttons on KCC's shirt so I can see more of his chest hair. He pulls off his shirt before removing Brandon's.

KCC grabs the back of my neck and pushes his tongue into my mouth. Brandon pulls KCC's head back and gives a long, hard lick to his neck. KCC grunts. Brandon does the same to me as KCC and I kiss. I groan into KCC's mouth.

KCC and Brandon have my shirt off before I can object. I don't want them to see me without it and get turned off. I don't like my soft tummy. I shouldn't worry. They do. Their hands stroke and grab at me. They kiss my body. Their mouths feel good.

As much as I want to enjoy the moment, my thoughts are interrupting. I keep thinking about putting my shirt back on. I keep thinking about how I can please KCC and Brandon. I wonder if they like what I'm doing to them. Then the voice inside me reminds me about Mama Bear's and Di's warnings. I start to wonder what's going to happen next, what KCC and Brandon expect me to do. My stomach clenches. I'm not sure how much further I want to go. I'm not sure I'm ready. I freeze up.

"What's up?" Brandon asks.

"Nothing," I say. "I'm shy." I cover my stomach with my arms. It's not exactly a lie. I don't know how to tell them I'm nervous about how this celebration is progressing.

"You're a hot little cub. Don't worry," KCC says, pulling my arms away and licking my nipple before kissing down toward my belly button.

I blurt out, "Is it okay if we slow down?"

"What, aren't you enjoying this?" KCC asks.

Brandon and KCC kiss each other again.

My stomach lurches, and my head sways like I'm dizzy. "I am. But it's all happening so fast," I reply.

"You need to relax, cub. Go with it," Brandon says. "You earned it. Aren't you having fun?"

He sucks on my earlobe. I quiver against him. "Yes," I say. "I am."

"You're in a great position," KCC says as he rubs the back of my head again. He kisses my jaw softly. "You'll win, get the job and have some fun with us in the process. We can guarantee you a career and help you open your little bakery. Don't you want that?"

"I do," I say. I kiss KCC softly on the lips. "I just need a little break."

KCC kisses me hard, aggressively, like he kissed Brandon. He pinches my nipple and bites my lip.

I push him away. "Ow. That hurt."

KCC smirks. "It should always hurt a little the first time," he says.

I push him away again.

"Relax," Brandon repeats. "We're having fun." He slides his hand up my thigh and undoes the button on my jeans.

I push his hand away too.

"I want to stop," I say. I try to stand up, but I'm stuck under them.

"You don't want to ruin your chances, do you?" KCC asks. He slides his hand down my pants and squeezes me. "See? I knew you were liking this."

I try to pull his hand off. I can't make it budge. "Stop. Please," I say as the door to the office opens.

Mama Bear, out of drag, walks in. "Am I interrupting?" he asks as he sees the three of us.

"What do you think?" KCC says. He pulls his hand out of my pants and flings himself back into the couch.

Brandon slides his arm around my shoulders and pulls me into him. "What do you want, Bear?"

"I came to discuss next week. Looks like you guys are already figuring it out." Mama Bear looks at me and me only.

I do up my pants, then grab my shirt off the floor. Brandon's arm drops from my shoulders.

"He wanted to stop," Mama Bear says.

KCC huffs. "It was only some fun."

"Theo?" Mama Bear asks. "You okay?"

I nod.

Mama Bear keeps eye contact with me.

KCC adds, "He was into it. You liked it, didn't you, cub?"

"At first," I admit.

"Don't be a baby. Admit you wanted it," KCC says.

"He's seventeen," Mama Bear says.

His eyes are still locked on mine.

"Christ. Why would you tell me that now?" KCC asks, his voice changing from smooth to sharp.

"Maybe you should have reviewed the applications," Mama Bear says.

"Are you trying to suggest something?" KCC asks, his tone getting sharper. "We haven't done anything wrong."

"Haven't you?" Mama Bear asks.

"Don't make me out to be the bad guy. The cub knew what he was doing when he hit on us. No one forced him to come into my office. He knew what he wanted and what he'd do to get it," KCC says.

"What?" I say. "It isn't like that. I like you two, but it was all going really fast. And there's two of you, and you're both older and married."

"You knew that and you still came in here," KCC replies. "Don't pretend you weren't drooling all over me from the moment we met."

"He's been playing us," Brandon says. He looks at KCC. "It's obvious. He's just trying to get ahead."

"Is that the story you're going with?" Mama Bear asks. "That this teenage cub is trying to play you two?"

"He was liking everything before you came in," Brandon says with a shrug. "Who knows what he'd do to win. KCC's a big name. Maybe he was planning on accusing us of something."

Brandon and KCC nod at one another.

"He's using us," KCC says. "It's clear. He tried to play us. He's not some immature, inexperienced kid. He's out to get what he wants however he has to."

"KCC?" I say. "I was having a good time. Really. I like you two. If you let me explain, we could figure things out."

KCC turns away from me. "I think we've got you figured out. Get out. Both of you," he orders. I don't move, so he says, "Now. Go on, get off my couch and get out of here. You had your chance. You ruined it."

"KCC?" I say again as I stand. "Brandon?"

"We could have helped you. A lot," KCC says as I make my way out the door. "I thought you knew what you wanted. I thought you had priorities. You knew what you were in for. I figured you were a big slut. I didn't realize you were a stupid slut. Get your fat ass out of my restaurant."

Chapter Ten

Mama Bear insists on driving me home. His car looks like it was made from leftovers of other cars. Every piece is a different color. The only unifying feature is the rust.

We don't talk on the ride. Mama Bear glances at me every time he checks the mirrors. Maybe he's expecting me to cry, but my eyes feel dry. I don't feel much of anything. I keep replaying the events in my head.

I am so relieved that Mama Bear came in when he did. A part of me, the part making my stomach grind, knows that if KCC and Brandon had just slowed down a little, I probably would have done whatever they wanted. I liked how hot they were, how they found me attractive, how they wanted me, how they told me I was talented and could win. I even enjoyed the physical stuff. So I went along with it. I guess I really am a big, stupid, fat slut.

Mama Bear pulls over near my place. "What's going on in there?" he asks.

I don't know how to answer.

"Listen," Mama Bear says. "KCC is a huge dick. He shouldn't have put you in that situation. You shouldn't have had to tell him to stop. He shouldn't have started. What KCC and Brandon tried is wrong."

I shake my head. "I was a willing participant. Di warned me. You warned me. But they were nice to me. They offered to help me. I thought they actually cared about me."

"They hurt you," Mama Bear says. "It doesn't matter if KCC is God's gift to gays or even God himself. He doesn't get to treat you like crap and then blame you for what he did."

"I guess."

Mama Bear heaves a big sigh. "You can only try to trust better guys in the future. Guys who treat you well. Guys who are nice to you and don't expect anything in return. You don't need to waste your time on assholes you can find anywhere, anytime. KCC's not special. *You* are. Don't forget that."

"I'm not though," I say. "What KCC said was right."

Mama Bear unbuckles his seat belt and leans over to hug me. His body is warm and soft. He doesn't let go. I rest my head on his shoulder and curl into him.

"KCC is wrong. You're a great cook. You don't make people feel like garbage. And maybe you don't see it, but you're cute as anything." Mama Bear strokes the back of my head and keeps hugging me.

I feel small and safe. I turn my head and look at him. He looks good in a lumberjack way with his big beard. Maybe I did pick wrong. Maybe I missed a good guy right in front of me because of how awestruck I was over KCC. Maybe I should have taken a chance on a different guy.

I lift my head up to kiss Mama Bear. I lean in. Our lips nearly touch.

Mama Bear pulls back. "I'm sorry. I don't think that's a good idea."

"What? Why?" I sit back in my seat and feel my cheeks start to burn.

"I thought…you said pick a better guy. You called me cute."

"You are," Mama Bear says. "But I have to actually *be* a better guy, and you're making that really hard." He gives a big sigh and closes his eyes, pinching the bridge of his nose. "KCC and Brandon are too old for you. I am too. You're upset, and it wouldn't be right. I'd be taking advantage."

"You don't want to kiss me?" I ask.

"What I want doesn't matter," Mama Bear says. "If you were a little older or I was a little younger, it would be different."

"I'm not that young."

"You're still in high school. We're in different places. I'm sorry, Theo. I know this feels shitty, but don't take it as a rejection."

"It is a rejection." I unlock my door and grasp my backpack. "Thanks for the ride."

Mama Bear grabs hold of my hand as I get out of the car. "I'll call you. I didn't mean to make you feel bad. But trust me, it's better this way. Especially for you."

"Right." I slam the door and walk away.

I don't want Mama Bear to call. I don't want KCC or Brandon to call either. I want a voice mail from the ditzy guy telling me I've been cut from HEAT's competition. After making it to the finals and then being dropped by KCC, Brandon and Mama Bear, all in the span of a few hours, I don't think I can face any of them again. If I'm not kicked out of the contest, I'll have to quit.

Chapter Eleven

"I called you twenty-three times in a row," Mama Bear says. "I was wondering how many it would take before you blocked me. I left messages until your box was full."

"I've been busy," I say. "You know, with high school."

Mama Bear doesn't take the bait. "How are you doing?"

"I'm fine," I say. After he dropped me off, I went inside and ate a tub of ice cream. That only made me feel worse, so I ran around the block until I threw up in my neighbor's bushes. Sadly, I didn't even do that many laps. "If you called for anything else, like to tell me I'm out of the contest, don't worry. I've already decided I can't go back to HEAT."

There's silence.

"Is something wrong?" I ask.

"Just you," Mama Bear says. "You don't see that right now you have all the power. Zack's posting has made this competition huge. HEAT is making loads of money and getting a lot of press. You've got a massive fan following. KCC *can't* cut you. He's hoping you won't show up. He wants you to forfeit. He's ready to throw Dixon, Jeff and Dennis back in and extend the competition. It would take all three of them and the extra weeks to replace you."

"I don't have any power. KCC won't let me win even if I do come back."

Mama Bear says, "Do you want KCC to have the last word?"

"It's his competition. At his restaurant. He automatically has the last word. Besides, you heard what he said to me," I say. "Anyway, I have to go."

"Wait," Mama Bear says. "Whether you come back or not, I'm going to keep calling you to see how you're doing."

"I can't stop you."

"Theo, there's something else you should know that may change your mind. The final round is dessert."

Oh crap.

"I get why you might want to drop out and how embarrassed you must feel," Mama Bear continues. "But you have a chance to show everyone, including KCC, that you have what it takes. You're the baker cub. Even Chef KCC can only cook. Why not make KCC choke on that? You're better than him, and not just because you're a better baker."

"I'll think about it," I say before we hang up.

"Was that about the contest?" Di asks. I was in the sewing lab with her when Mama Bear began blowing up my phone. Di's wearing what I can only describe as a metallic jester outfit. Her sleeves keep getting in the way of the sewing machine.

I nod and tell Di what Mama Bear said. She listens as she sews.

"What do you want to do?" she asks.

"I don't know. Since you're always right, I was hoping you'd tell me," I say.

She shakes her head. "This one has to be your call. If you don't want to go back, I get that. And if you do, I get that too."

"Come on, Di. You love to tell me what to do!"

"This one has to be you. You have to decide for yourself," she says.

"I don't want to see any of them again," I say. "All I've been is humiliated and ashamed. I know maybe it wasn't all my fault, but you were right about them being too old for me. About the whole thing being a bad idea."

"You took a chance. You were adventurous. You shouldn't be ashamed. You didn't do anything wrong," Di says.

We sit in silence. Di keeps sewing.

I sigh. "It's dessert. That's my thing. But what if it's a trick?"

"This isn't about dessert or the final round. This is about who you are. You're a baker. No one, not even KCC, should scare you off your own turf." Di pulls the fabric from the sewing machine.

"Then I don't have any other choice. I have to go back. And I have to bake," I say.

"You'll want to wear this when you do." Di hands me what she's been working on.

I get to HEAT and head straight to my station to see what equipment is there. I brought a couple of extra things just in case. On my way to the backstage area, KCC corners me. I freeze when I see him. I remember freezing in his office.

"We should talk," he says.

I don't answer.

"Listen. Things got crazy in the heat of the moment."

"I agree," I manage to get out.

"But I'm glad you're here." KCC gives me a smile. It's a great smile.

He sounds smooth again. He still smells great, still looks handsome.

I hate myself for thinking that.

"I want things to be good between us. Brandon and I talked. We should all hang out. No drama this time."

"I don't know…" I say.

KCC reaches out and rubs my forearm. "We can make sure you win. And we'll get you a good job to start you out. We can give you everything you want. That includes us." He smiles again. The light catches his teeth and shines. He looks sexy. He's being nice like he was that time he drove me home. "It's a good offer, cub. You should take it."

I remind myself that no matter how good KCC looks or smells or acts, I left his office feeling horrible about myself. I won't give him another chance to make me feel that way again.

"No, thanks," I say. "I don't want the win if you're handing it to me.

I'm a baker. A real one. If I can't win fair and square, I don't deserve to."

"I see," KCC says. He crosses his arms over his chest. His smile is gone. "That's not the best business decision."

"Maybe not."

"Let's see if you still feel this way after tonight," he says and strides away.

I avoid him, Brandon and Mama Bear as they all hurry around the restaurant before start time. I can't be thinking about any of them now. I have lots of work ahead of me. I even made a time schedule for myself. I have to focus on the baking and only the baking.

When Mama Bear announces my name I walk out to my station. The lights are brighter than normal. I start to sweat instantly. In the audience I see Di sitting next to Benji. None of his friends are at their table. I look down at the apron Di made for me. On the front she has created a bear's head out of fake fur, teeth bared, roaring. She even sewed me matching bear-paw oven mitts with claws. I feel like a warrior dressed for battle.

Arm raised, Mama Bear looks at Zack and me.

"Okay, boys, for the last time, Ready, Set, HEAT!"

I grab my schedule, my list and my mixing bowls and arrange them on the counter. I then start placing all the ingredients I will need on a cookie sheet so I don't forget any as I go.

KCC stops at my station. "You're wasting valuable time," he says.

I ignore him. Once I'm organized, I begin to weigh my ingredients.

"A little too hot in here, big boy?" KCC says quietly, so only I can hear. He pretends to inspect the contents of my bowls. "Maybe you need to slow down. Stop. Take a break. *Please.*"

I continue to ignore him. He moves on.

Soon my station is smelling delicious as I move pans in and out of the oven. My mixers whip nonstop.

"My offer is still good," KCC whispers. He has reappeared behind me. I can smell his cologne. I close my eyes and breathe it in. He touches my lower back.

I could lean into him a little. I could guarantee a win instead of fighting so hard for what is almost sure to be a loss.

"We both know you don't need to bake to get me out of my pants, cub," he says smoothly. "What will it take to get you out of yours?"

I step away. I slip on my oven mitts and use my new paws to grab a hot tray. As I bend over, KCC squeezes my ass.

I straighten up quickly. The bear's head on my apron shifts and roars across my chest. I step back onto KCC's foot.

With a muttered curse KCC pulls his foot out from under mine. He leans in closer. "I'm getting tired of you playing hard to get, cub. I'm not afraid to play hard too."

I don't answer. I have five minutes left. I begin to add the decorations to my dessert. In the last minute, I clean the edges of the platters. As the crowd counts down the final seconds, I wipe my brow and stand back, happy with what I've done. Even if it doesn't win, I know it's a winning dessert.

Mama Bear introduces KCC and Brandon to the crowd. But there is one more judge.

"We have a special guest judge for the dessert round. If you haven't tried her sweet treats, you don't know what you're missing. Seriously, what have you been doing? Her stores are everywhere in this city. Please welcome Trudy Singh, *the* Trudy behind Truly Trudy Bake Shoppes."

A woman steps into the light. She looks sweet in a '50s-style party dress with chocolate-chip cookies and glasses of milk all over it. She has paired it with brightly colored high-tops. With a friendly grin on her face, she ruffles KCC's and Brandon's hair as she takes her place at the table.

Up first, Zack presents a beautiful pavlova with passion fruit curd. The judges agree that it's delicious, with a layered profile. Creamy, crunchy, marshmallowy, tart. He scores two eights and a seven, for a total of twenty-three points.

The servers carry my platters to the judges.

"Tell me about your dessert, Theo?" Trudy asks, smiling down at my dessert. Her fork is ready in her hand.

"It's a tasting plate. In front of you there are a dozen mini cupcakes. Each one is different. There is a classic vanilla and a chocolate, but also candied maple bacon, green tea and blond chocolate and a lot more in between. All of them can be eaten in a single bite. I call them 'cubcakes.'" While Trudy smiles at this, I notice KCC's eyes narrowing. There's no going back now.

"You can eat them in any order," I continue, "but I suggest starting at the top and going clockwise. That way you can experience a unique and deliberate flavor journey as you go."

Trudy puts down her fork. She plucks up the first cubcake and pops it into her mouth. She closes her eyes as she chews. A smile spreads across her face.

The audience murmurs in excitement.

"It's way too much," Brandon says, partway through his platter. He pushes it away.

"Exactly. Far too much sweetness," KCC agrees. "Who would even eat all this?"

Trudy opens her eyes. "I would. Do you realize how tough it would be to make all these in the time given? I think it is the ultimate dessert. It's decadent. It's sublime." She licks some frosting off her pinkie finger. "It's a perfect ten."

Brandon and KCC whisper to one another. They give me a five and a six. Despite the perfect score from Trudy, I lose by two points.

Chapter Twelve

Zack comes over to me right after he is announced the winner.

"Your dessert was better than mine," he says before the crowd surrounds him. "I don't even need to taste it to know. My feed is going insane. Everyone is saying you should have won, and I agree. I'm sorry, man."

I shake Zack's hand. "Congratulations," is all I say.

Other people come up to me too. Some offer condolences. Some tell me I was robbed. Some ask me if I do special orders and ask for my card. But soon the crowd dies down. I tell Di to wait for me. I go to the bathroom to wash my face.

I expected to feel worse. But my stomach isn't complaining anymore. In fact, I feel light, maybe even a bit relieved, as I splash water on my face. Trudy Singh, the queen of bakeries, gave me a perfect score. I know my cubcakes were great. They showed off my skills and creativity and ambition, and Trudy saw that. I'm proud of them. I'm even a little proud of myself.

As I pat my forehead dry, the bathroom door opens. KCC smirks as he closes it behind him and locks it.

"Have you reconsidered anything since our earlier chat?" he asks.

I pat my jaw dry. I don't make eye contact.

"I thought you might have after your big loss. Your dessert was the best. I know that. You know that. But you needed to learn a business lesson. Make friends, not enemies. You should thank me for that."

"Thanks then," I say, eyes on the floor.

He's blocking the door. "I can make or break you, cub. Is that what you want?"

I lift my gaze. "I'm still figuring out what I want," I say. I keep staring him in the eyes. "I do know that I don't want to be used by two grown, married men though. I'm still a kid, after all, and it's just food."

"You're so much stupider than I thought," KCC says, unlocking the door.

I shrug. "But I'm not a slut." I keep staring at him.

"Whatever. Your fat ass is not worth it." KCC walks out.

I throw the paper towel away and leave too. I see KCC and Brandon talking to Zack by the cooking stations. They're probably congratulating him. I see Brandon rub Zack's shoulder. KCC steps closer to Zack and says something in his ear. KCC turns his head and looks at me as he whispers. Zack giggles and slaps KCC on the shoulder playfully.

I want to warn Zack, but I can't exactly walk over there and tell him my story right now. Would he even listen to me if I did? I didn't listen to Di or Mama Bear. Zack and I make eye contact. I shake my head as I get my phone out to text him a warning. Zack gives a tiny wink before turning back to KCC and Brandon. Zack's arm twitches. I look down and see him tapping his phone, a red light blinking under his fingertip.

He'll be okay.

"You were great tonight," Di says. She links arms with me. Tonight she's in a summer dress, white with black and gold bees flying all over it. She looks underdressed compared to her normal style, but she doesn't need anything else.

"Thanks to your apron," I say.

"You didn't need the apron. I hate to tell you this, but your confidence was showing."

"Better than my ass," I say with a laugh.

"Oh, that was showing too. Benji didn't miss it once."

"Whatever, hag," I say. We are laughing as we leave the restaurant.

Mama Bear rushes out after us. "Glad I caught you!" he says.

"Can we talk later?" I ask. "I am wiped. I promise I'll pick up when you call."

"It can't wait," Mama Bear says. "Trudy Singh is insisting."

Just then Trudy steps out of HEAT. She walks over to us and shakes my hand. "Theo, I completely disagree with tonight's decision. I can't change it. Believe me, I tried. But I can ask you if you would apprentice for me. It won't be a paid job. But it would look good on your culinary-school application, and it would be a great learning experience. You're a remarkable baker. I'd love to work with you. I hope you will consider it."

"I don't need to consider it," I say without hesitation. "I would love to, thank you!"

Trudy smiles and pats my arm. "Mama Bear will give me your information. I'll be in touch. And Theo?"

"Yes?"

"You're going to have to share your recipes with me. I finished off KCC's and Brandon's platters. I can't stop thinking about those cubcakes."

"He gets that a lot," Di says. "You should try his soy-caramel brownies."

I kind of hate to admit it, but as far as hags go, mine is the greatest.

Mama Bear and Trudy go back into HEAT. Di and I head to the subway. "I can't believe the night I had," I say. "But I'm starving. Let's grab a dog, and I'll fill you in on what you missed."

"Yeah, I'm hungry too. And I'm not happy I didn't get any of those cubcakes. To make up for it, you're treating. And don't think for a second I'll give up until I get my own platter," says Di.

We walk to the hot-dog vendor around the corner. As I'm paying, I hear, "Hey, Theo." I turn around to see Benji. He comes up beside me and orders a hot dog.

"You were awesome tonight," he says. "Like usual." He laughs that barking laugh again. He blushes. It's still cute and surprising.

"But I lost," I say.

"Zack has all those followers. It was politics," Benji says.

"Something like that," Di says as she loads up her hot dog with toppings. "I hate to do this, Theo, but I have a new outfit I need to work on. It can't wait. I've got to go."

"At least stay and eat with me," I say.

"Sorry, can't," she answers as she hurries away.

I stand there waiting for my hot dog.

"I'll stay," Benji offers. His arm brushes against mine.

Benji and I get our hot dogs and drinks. I see a low stone wall nearby. We sit. We start to talk about the contest. We start to talk about school. We start to talk about our friends. I tell him about Di and her fashion. He tells me about his friends' styles. I think he's adorable enough to land any one of them. Except here he is with me.

This time I'm sure of Benji's interest. Even if I weren't, I'm sure of mine. He's sweet and cute and laughs like a dork, and I like that. I'd be stupid not to take a chance.

I reach for Benji's hand. He looks down, surprised. I start to let go, but Benji squeezes back. He laughs again. I laugh too. I don't let go of his hand. He leans into me, and I lean into him. My heart beats fast, and suddenly I feel out of breath. Our lips gently touch. The kiss lasts only a few seconds.

I rest my forehead against his as I try to slow my heart and catch my breath. He has a faint spray of freckles across his nose, so light they almost blend in. Benji is breathing hard too. It tickles. He smells clean and new, like fresh laundry.

I lick my lips. They taste sweet, but there's something else there. I can't quite place it. It leaves me wanting more.

So I kiss him again.

Acknowledgments

I would like to express my heartfelt gratitude to the following people:

Tanya Trafford, for taking a chance on me and Theo. She knew exactly what was needed (those secret editor's ingredients that take things to the next level). Thanks to the rest of the team at Orca Book Publishers too, for helping me transform from someone who writes into an actual author.

Brooke Carter, an amazing writer and friend who selflessly kicked open a publishing door for me, patiently answered all my questions and offered advice, and is too humble and cool to take the credit she deserves.

Susan Juby, for being a mentor in the best ways, for her brilliance, and for asking me to contribute to her blog, which helped lead me here.

Sarah Tsiang and Maggie de Vries, for all their help, friendship and support.

All my friends, especially Claudia, Kristin, Kevin, Julia, Justin, Anita, François, Amanda, Mary, and Jennifer Coffey, who is a true writer but an even truer friend.

My family, immediate and extended, for everything they gave with no expectations and who never hesitated to encourage, support, and believe in me. What I give to my writing, I got from all of you in some way first.

It hardly seems like enough, but thank you.

Paul Coccia has an MFA in Creative Writing from UBC. He is a great cook, although he prefers to bake. His specialty is cupcakes, but he has also experimented with animal-shaped macarons and flooded cookies. Paul lives in Toronto, Ontario, with his family and two dogs. *Cub* is his first novel.

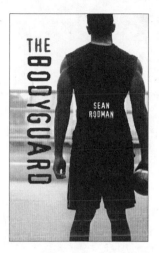

9781459822016 PB

Ryan Hale, aka "Replay," is the greatest running back in the history of his high school football team, despite the fact that he would much rather be behind his camera, making movies. To earn some money, he agrees to act as bodyguard for Markus, a strange exchange student with outrageous stories about mobsters and hackers.

Chapter One

My name is Ryan "Replay" Hale. According to the local newspaper, I'm the greatest running back that Marathon High School has ever seen. The *Marathon Tribune* called me a "talent to watch." And "the golden boy of the Golden Warriors."

But they don't know about my pregame ritual—barfing quietly in a locker-room bathroom stall, hoping nobody hears me. The only one who does hear me, unfortunately, is my best friend, Alex. He always stands guard outside.

"Replay?" he hisses through the stall door. "You almost finished? Game time in five."

My empty stomach lurches again, trying to hurl whatever might be left down there into the stained toilet bowl in front of me. The result of a nasty cocktail of nerves and fear. Not for the first time I wonder at the cruel joke of genetics that made me into a football superman. I'd much prefer to be Clark Kent. I have a love-hate thing with the game of football.

I'm distracted from my misery by muffled voices outside the stall door.

"Replay must have had a bad burrito, Coach," I overhear Alex say. "No big deal, sir. He'll be right out."

Alex thumps on the door. "Seriously, man! Ride the vomit comet and get out here."

There's no more putting it off. I can't disappoint Alex. My team. My parents. I wipe my mouth with the back of a gloved hand and adjust my neck roll. My stomach feels like it's filled with battery acid. But it's time for my game face. I slide my helmet on, hoping it will hide my seasick expression, and open the stall door.

"Replay! Good to see you, man!" Alex checks his watch and raises an eyebrow. "Seventeen minutes and thirty-seven seconds of solid puke." His teeth flash white as he grins and slaps me on my shoulder pads. We walk out of the locker room and through the dim tunnel toward the brightly lit field. He's chuckling to himself all the way.

"What are you so happy about?" I ask. As we step out of the tunnel, the noise and sights of the field make Alex pause before answering. The big screen is flashing a pre-game show, throwing crazy shadows everywhere. The stands are like rippling sheets of gold, Warriors fans decked out in our school colors. It feels like a circus with the drums banging away and cheerleaders spinning and twirling, all blond hair and wide smiles.

We walk over to our place on the bench. It's occupied by a new guy, a freshman. Alex gives him the hard stare until he shoves over. Star treatment for the star players, like me and him. I guess football has some perks.

"Why am I happy, you ask? Well, I'm proud of you, son." Alex puts a fatherly hand on my shoulder.

"Proud of me? For what?"

"That was your personal best for a pregame spew-fest. The more you barf, the better you play. I've watched you do this for what, a dozen games?" He gives me a toothy grin. "Bet you didn't know this, but I timed all your barf-o-thons."

"That's actually kinda creepy."

"No, no. I'm a scientist, man. I have the data to back me up now. It's not just a theory. Longer barf session equals better game performance. It's a fact. You're going to be awesome on the field tonight." Alex suddenly looks serious and leans in toward me. The crowd roars louder. "Just don't lose your lunch while you're wearing your helmet. That'll get ugly."

"Thanks for the advice, man." Time for the other part of my pre-game ritual. I pull out a small video camera from my backpack under the bench. "Also, how come you know so many words for 'puke'? How many can there be?"

orca soundings

For more information on all the books
in the Orca Soundings series, please visit
orcabook.com.